ORCHARD

# Ballet Stories for Young Children

Saviour Pirotta
Brigette Barrager

For Martha
S.P.

To all the Dreamers and Dancers
B.B.

ORCHARD BOOKS

First published in Great Britain in 2016 by The Watts Publishing Group

1 3 5 7 9 10 8 6 4 2



A CIP catalogue record for this book is available from the British Library.

ISBN 978 1 40830 313 9

Printed and bound in China

Orchard Books
An imprint of Hachette Children's Group
Part of The Watts Publishing Group Limited
Carmelite House, 50 Victoria Embankment, London EC4Y 0DZ

An Hachette UK Company
www.hachette.co.uk

www.hachettechildrens.co.uk

This book belongs to

# Contents

This book belongs to

# Contents

A CELEBRATION WAS TAKING PLACE at King Floristan's palace: a christening party for his daughter, the Princess Aurora, who was named after the beauty of the dawn.

All the guests in the grand ballroom gathered round the crib as six fairies showered the princess with magic gifts.

"I give her the gift of honesty."

"And I, happiness."

"I bestow upon her grace."

"Mine is the gift of song."

"And mine, kindness."

Last of all came the Lilac Fairy, who was the wisest and most powerful fairy of all. "My gift shall be—"

Her words were cut short by guards shouting at the

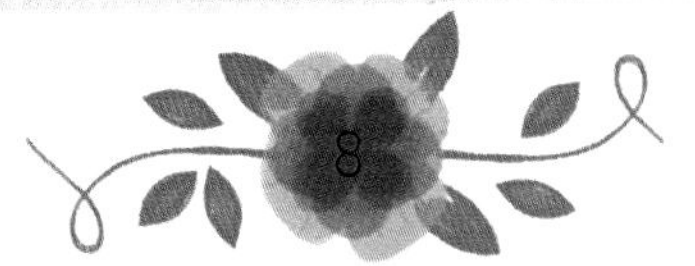

door. Someone had broken into the palace! A hideous coach, shaped like a snarling black cat, came thundering into the ballroom, pulled by six enormous rats. A shadow as deep as night unfolded, and out stepped Carabosse, the evil fairy.

"A grand party for the little one, I see," she said, glaring at King Floristan and the queen with eyes as hard as diamonds. "What a shame not to be invited . . . "

The king's master of ceremonies stepped forward to

protect the baby's cradle. "It was my fault, your ladyship," he stammered. "I must have mislaid the invitation."

"Mislaid the invitation? How clumsy of you!" Carabosse snapped her fingers and the man's wig flew off his head. Everyone gasped, and the evil fairy turned to King Floristan. "I couldn't possibly NOT give the new princess a gift," she cackled.

Carabosse approached the princess. Stirring the air above the crib with her crooked walking stick, she said, "On her sixteenth birthday, the princess will prick her finger on the needle of a spinning wheel – and die!"

There was a flash of lightning that nearly hit the crib. Carabosse shrieked with laughter, and a moment later she was back in her coach and out of the ballroom, the cat-coach snarling fire.

The Lilac Fairy fluttered to Aurora's side. "Do not fret, Your Majesties," she said to the king and queen. "I have yet to bestow my own gift upon the princess. Carabosse's magic is too powerful even for me to stop. But I can soften it! My gift to the Princess Aurora is this: when she pricks her finger on the needle, she will not die. Instead, she will fall asleep for one hundred years, to be woken only by her true love's kiss."

Sixteen years passed in which Princess Aurora grew up to be everything the fairies had decreed she would be: honest, graceful, musical, happy, and kind to everyone she met. And she never once pricked or cut her finger on a needle, for her father had every spinning wheel banned from the kingdom.

For Aurora's sixteenth birthday, the king organised a ball in the palace garden. Only nobles and fairies had been invited to the christening, but this celebration was

to be different. Everyone from the surrounding villages was invited, no matter who they were.

The guests all brought gifts for the princess: warm blankets, fresh fruit and delicious cakes. An old woman in a woollen shawl pulled the princess aside and pressed something into her hands.

"What is this?" asked Aurora.

"Have you never seen one of these before?" said the old lady.

"Never," replied the princess. "What is it for?"

"Dance with it round the garden and you'll see," suggested the old lady.

Aurora clasped the strange object to her chest and started dancing, whirling from one friend to another. "See, everyone. That kind old lady gave me something I have never seen before."

Looking up, the queen saw the object in Aurora's hand and went suddenly pale. "Aurora . . . "

But it was too late. The princess stopped dead in her tracks, holding out a trembling

hand. A drop of blood was welling up on her finger, as round and bright as a ladybird.

The old woman threw off her shawl and roared with laughter. She was none other than the wicked Carabosse in disguise, and the gift she'd pressed on Aurora was . . . a spindle from a spinning wheel.

"At last, Princess," she cackled, "my wish for you has come true." Then she disappeared in a flash of smoke.

No sooner was she gone than Princess Aurora fell to the ground. The king and queen rushed to their daughter's side, but it was no use. She seemed to be dead.

"Not dead," whispered a voice as faint as the summer breeze. "She is sleeping. Only sleeping, remember? Sleeping peacefully for one hundred years . . . "

By now the sun was setting. The Lilac Fairy flitted around the garden, waving her silver wand. She rose up into the sky and, as she did, everyone in the castle fell gently asleep: men and women, grown-ups and children, even the animals and the fish in the streams.

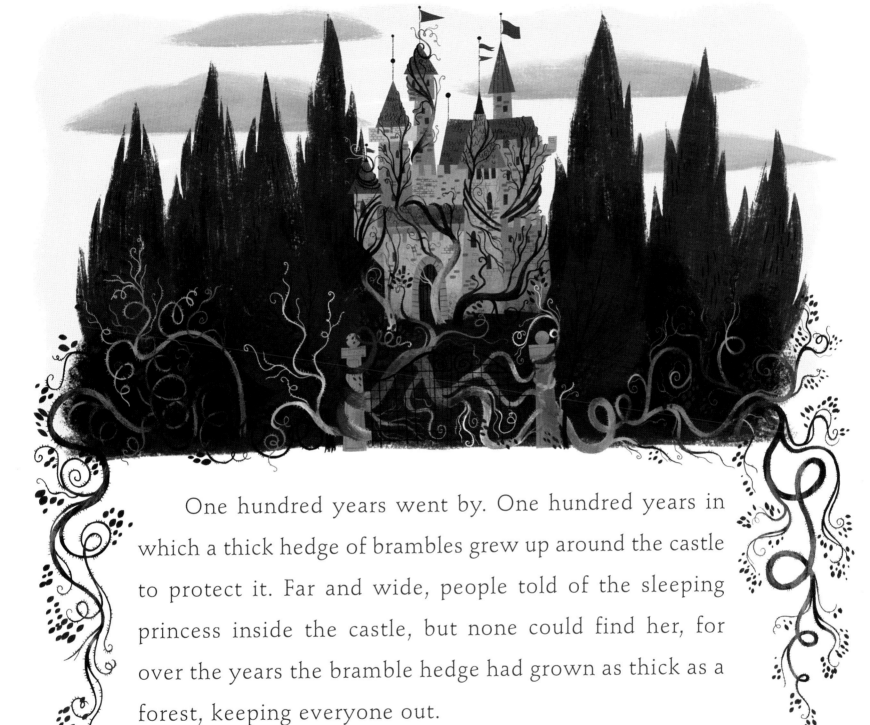

One hundred years went by. One hundred years in which a thick hedge of brambles grew up around the castle to protect it. Far and wide, people told of the sleeping princess inside the castle, but none could find her, for over the years the bramble hedge had grown as thick as a forest, keeping everyone out.

Then one day a prince came to the edge of a thorny forest. He'd been riding with his friends but, somehow

he'd got lost. He was tired too, for night after night a strange dream had kept him awake.

The prince stopped under a tree to rest. He fell asleep, and once more he had the mysterious dream, in which he saw a beautiful princess asleep on a velvet cot. She was so beautiful he could not help but kiss her gently on the lips. In his dream, the princess trembled and her hand flew to her lips, as if to seal the kiss to them for ever. Then she opened her eyes . . .

Usually the dream ended there, but today it continued. A fairy, dressed in shimmering lilac, appeared above the prince's head.

"Prince Florimund . . . "

"Yes?"

"Do you love her?"

"I love her."

"She has been cursed to sleep for one hundred years, waiting for her prince. Only true love will wake her. Do you wish to find her?"

"I wish for nothing more in the world."

"Then open your eyes. The one hundred years are drawing to an end . . . "

The prince woke up to find himself deeper in the forest. He picked up his sword, and, slashing his way through the brambles, arrived outside a castle. There were guards snoring on the steps, and pageboys asleep inside the door.

A flickering light, the colour of lilac, guided him on. He walked down long, dusty corridors and across vast halls where lords and ladies sat asleep in their chairs.

Up a narrow flight of stairs he went, through curtains of mildewed cobwebs, to a jewelled door.

The prince pushed it open and there was the princess of his dreams, asleep on her velvet cot. Just as he had done in the dream, he tiptoed to her side and kissed her gently on the lips.

Aurora's eyes fluttered open and her hand flew to her lips. "My prince! How long have I been asleep?"

"One hundred years," replied the prince. "But now it

is time to get up!"

Down in the grand hall, the king and the queen yawned and stretched. The guards stirred and the pageboys leapt to their feet. The prince led Aurora down to the ballroom, where her parents welcomed her with tears of joy.

"Princess, you are awake."

"You are safe."

The Lilac Fairy waved her wand and the thorny forest shrunk to nothing, letting the sun flood the castle with light and happiness. Happiest of all were Princess Aurora and Prince Florimund, for they both had found true love.

Their wedding was grander than Aurora's christening, grander even than her sixteenth birthday party, and this time there was no evil Carabosse with her wicked magic.

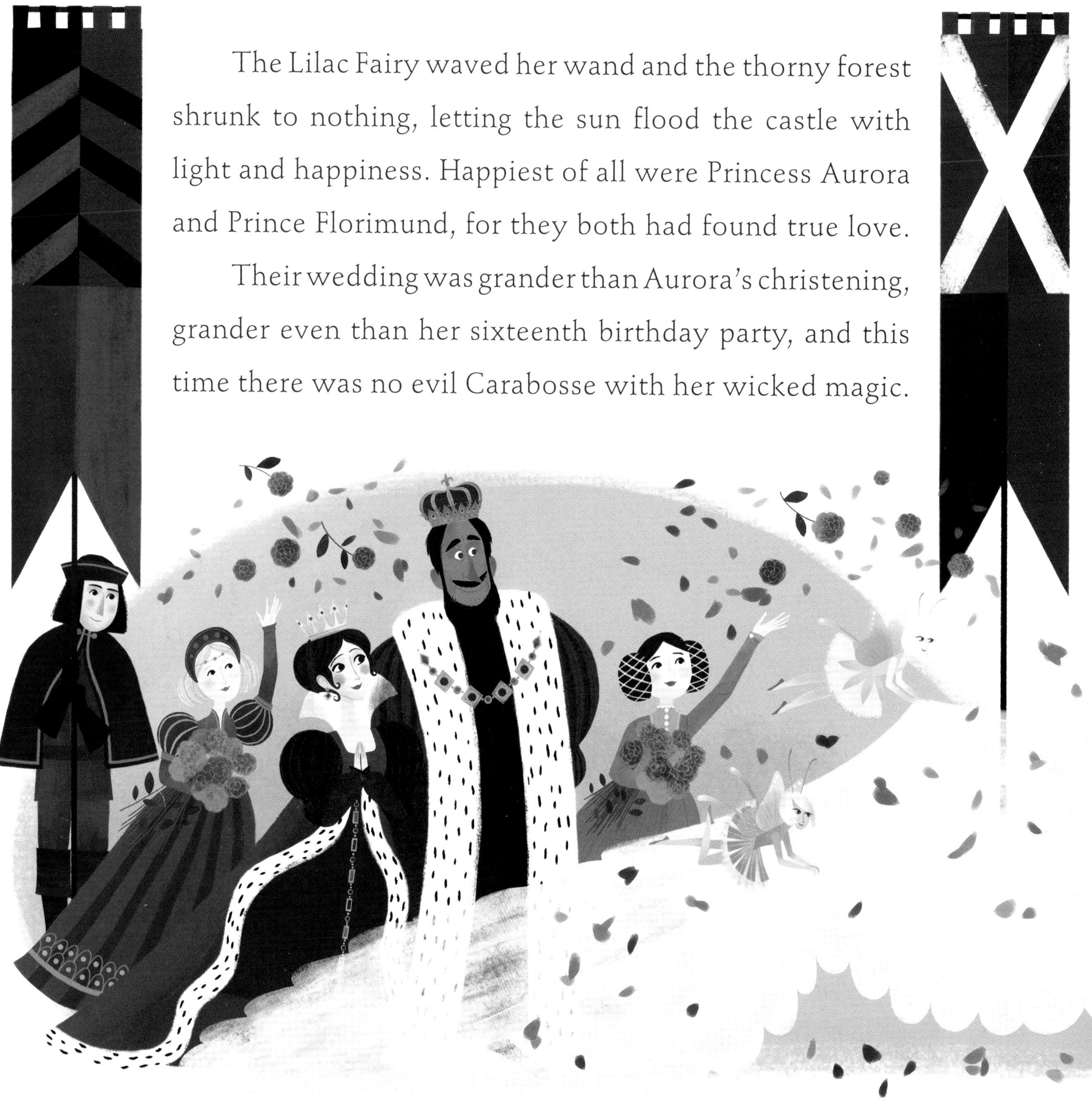

She had died a long time ago, leaving all the good fairies to bestow their magic gifts on everyone in the land.

# Coppelia

Doctor Coppelius lived right across the square from Swanilda. He was not the friendliest of neighbours. People said he was an inventor, but Swanilda had never seen anything he'd invented. He very rarely spoke to anyone and the windows to his workshop were always tightly shut.

There he was now, standing alone on his balcony

when everyone else was gathered in the town square.

"I feel almost sad for him," said Swanilda to her best friend. "He must not have any friends."

"Shush, you two," said Swanilda's boyfriend, Franz. "The mayor is about to give a speech."

"Ladies and gentlemen," said the mayor, holding up a fat purse, "tonight we are celebrating the new bells for the town hall. To mark the occasion, I promise that any couple who gets engaged tonight will have a share of this gold."

"Did you hear that, Franz?" said Swanilda's best friend. "You ought to propose to Swanilda today. You'll get enough gold to buy her a nice ring."

But neither Franz nor Swanilda was listening. They were both staring at Coppelius's balcony, where a beautiful girl had joined him. She was seated, reading a book.

"The old doctor has a visitor," said Swanilda. "I wonder who she is."

"She must be his niece," said her best friend.

"She's far too pretty to be Coppelius's niece," snorted Franz.

"Fancy sitting there reading while the mayor is giving a speech," said Swanilda. "How can she concentrate with all the noise?"

"Hello!" Franz called out to the girl. "What are you reading?"

"Stop that, Franz!" Swanilda fumed. "How dare you start talking to another girl while you're with me? It's embarrassing." And she folded her arms across her chest and stuck out her chin, just as she always did when she was angry. She even refused to join in when the mayor started the dancing.

Franz did join in, but he couldn't help throwing the odd glance up at Coppelius's balcony, making Swanilda angrier still. The mysterious girl never once looked up from her book. Eventually Coppelius led her back indoors, leaving the balcony door open. A moment later the doctor came out of the front door, alone. Franz and his friends crowded round him.

"Who's the young lady, doctor?"

"Will you introduce us to her?"

"Get out of my way," snarled Coppelius. "I'm late for my evening walk." He took off across the square, hitting out at the young men with his cane.

"Not very polite, is he?" laughed Swanilda. "I wonder if his visitor is more friendly."

"Look, he's dropped something," added her best friend, pointing to an object shining in the gutter. Swanilda picked it up.

"What is it?"

"A front door key, by the looks of it." Swanilda smiled. "Come on, let's take a peek inside Coppelius's house . . . "

"You wouldn't dare!" gasped her friends.

"We're not touching anything, only looking," said Swanilda. "I've often wondered what Coppelius does all day in that room at the top of the house. Besides, I want to see if this mysterious guest of his really is as pretty as Franz thinks."

Swanilda turned the key in the door and, one by one, her friends followed her inside, their hearts beating loud and fast. Coppelius's house was dark, with narrow stairs that led straight up to his workshop on the top floor.

"Hello? Is anyone there?" called Swanilda. There was no answer. She turned on a lamp – and her friends jumped. "Eeek!" The room was full of people, all sitting in chairs, their hands folded neatly on their laps.

"Good evening, everyone," said Swanilda nervously.

None of the figures replied or moved. Swanilda poked one of them gently in the shoulder. "They're only dolls!" she laughed. "Coppelius must have made them. Look, they have levers in their backs."

She pressed the lever on the doll she'd touched and it stood up. A smile appeared on its face, its eyes fluttered and it started dancing. Swanilda's friends set off the other dolls, and before long the room was full of twisting, twirling figures. One of them, a clown with golden hair, bumped into a wooden chest.

"I wonder what's in there," said Swanilda. She pulled the chest open and her eyes grew wide with mischief.

"Look, everyone, it's the mysterious girl from the balcony. She's a doll too. I can't wait to see Franz's face when I tell him . . . "

"Press her lever," Swanilda's best friend laughed.

But there was no time for any more pranks. Someone was coming up the stairs, their cane rattling along the banisters. Coppelius had returned. The girls fled, pushing past him down the stairs.

"Thieves! Vandals!" Coppelius shouted after them. "I ought to report you to the police."

In the workshop, Coppelius found his precious dolls scattered all over the floor, some still moving feebly as their clockwork wound down. He rushed straight to the chest by the window. Coppelia! Had the girls harmed his most precious creation? No, thank goodness, the chest was still closed.

A shadow fell across the balcony curtain, making Coppelius jump. Not another intruder! The doctor raised his cane to strike – and then he saw Franz. For a moment a scowl spread across his wrinkly face. But only for a moment. Then he grinned and lowered his cane.

"Good evening, young man."

Franz's jaw dropped when he saw Coppelius. "Doctor, I thought you were out. I meant no harm. It's just that I can't get your beautiful visitor out of my head."

"I don't blame you, sir," said Coppelius. "When a girl is that pretty, she is very hard to forget. Come in. Make yourself comfortable." He pulled out a chair for Franz.

"She'll be here in a moment, if you'd like me to introduce you. But let's have a drink while we're waiting. I have a special concoction I brew myself." He fetched glasses and poured the drink – a dark, foaming liquid.

"Go on, drink up," laughed Coppelius. "It will give you courage."

Franz took a swig. Ugh! The drink tasted horrible. A moment later his eyes started to water and the floor began to whirl under his feet. Then he collapsed in a heap.

Quickly, Coppelius laid Franz out on the chest where he kept Coppelia, making sure the young man's hands were folded neatly over his heart. Then he removed a floorboard and drew out an ancient leather-bound book. A book of spells!

"Only a moment longer, my precious Coppelia," whispered the doctor as he put the book on his worktable and opened it to the right page. "Only a moment longer and you shall come alive. Yes, your Uncle Coppelius has found a way to transfer this young man's life to you. You shall live and breathe, my dearest. You shall be a doll no more, but a real, live human being!"

Coppelius covered Franz's eyes with his hands and read out a spell. Franz's arms jerked and he moaned in his sleep. Another, longer, moan came from inside the chest.

"Coppelia!" The doctor pushed Franz to the floor and threw open the lid. Coppelia stood up. She looked around her, peering through the gloom with large, fluttering eyes.

Then she stepped out of the chest. She moved stiffly at first, just like a doll. But then she started dancing, and the more she danced, the less stiff she seemed, until in the end she was moving just like a real girl.

"My magic worked," cried Coppelius. "You're real!"

"Of course I am," replied the dancing girl. "But I am not your precious Coppelia."

"Not Coppelia?" said the doctor. "Then who are you?"

"Swanilda," laughed the girl. "And that man whose life you tried to steal is not dead. He is asleep. I hid in the chest while you were chasing my friends away and put on your Coppelia's clothes and wig."

"You cruel girl," cried Coppelius. "What did you do with my beloved Coppelia?"

"I stuffed her in the wardrobe," replied Swanilda.

Coppelius flung open the wardrobe, and there was Coppelia, lying in a tangled heap.

Franz opened his eyes and sat up shakily. "Where am I?"

"You are with me, darling," said Swanilda.

"Get out of my house," sobbed Coppelius. "You two have destroyed my life's work. It took me twenty years to make Coppelia and now she's ruined. Ruined beyond repair!"

"Come on, let's go, Swanilda," said Franz, getting to his feet. He wrapped his arms around her. "I'm sorry I was so rude to you, my dearest. I'll never look at another girl again."

"Or a doll?" Swanilda laughed.

"I promise," replied Franz.

The two of them ran down the stairs and out of the house, leaving Coppelius alone with his wrecked dolls. Their friends were still dancing in the square, and they joined them.

"So, has Franz proposed yet?" asked Swanilda's best friend.

"He has," replied Swanilda, "and I said yes. We're getting married tomorrow, right here on the steps of the town hall."

And that's what they did. Everyone in town was invited, even old Doctor Coppelius. Franz gave him the gold they got from the mayor, to make up for all the damage they had done to his dolls.

"Now I have enough money to build another Coppelia." The inventor smiled as Swanilda pulled him to his feet for a dance. "But I don't think I will. Who needs a doll when you can have real friends?"

# Swan Lake

SIEGFRIED WAS EVERY GIRL'S idea of a perfect prince. Tall, dark and handsome, he moved like a dancer and laughed loud and often. No wonder every princess dreamt of marrying him.

On his eighteenth birthday, Siegfried's mother, the queen, organised a grand ball. "Your father has invited every princess in Europe," she told Siegfried as

he celebrated with close friends in the palace garden. "We expect you to choose one of them for your wife." She turned to her son's tutor. "Don't you agree it's time for Siegfried to settle down, Wolfgang?"

"He would do well to obey your wishes, Your Majesty," muttered the tutor.

"I refuse to marry a princess simply because she is rich," protested Siegfried, "or because Father thinks her a suitable catch. I want to marry someone because I love them, and they love me."

"Princes do not marry for love," snapped the queen. "They marry to get richer and more powerful." She turned and marched back into the palace, leaving Siegfried to continue the celebrations with his companions.

"Don't look so glum," said Siegfried's friend Benno. "Let's have some party games."

"I don't feel like playing games," replied Siegfried. "I'm going for a walk. Walking always helps me think."

A flitting shadow passed across the garden and Siegfried looked up to see a flock of swans crossing the sky. He wondered where they were going.

"Shall I come with you?" asked Benno.

"No, you stay and enjoy the party," said Siegfried. "I'm only going to the woods." He threw a cloak round his shoulders and hurried out of the palace gates.

The sun had set by the time he reached the woods but he wasn't frightened. He came here often and knew the paths like the back of his hand. He kept walking until he came to the shores of a lake. There, gathered on the shore, were the swans he'd seen earlier. Some were still only cygnets with squat beaks.

One of the birds seemed to be wearing a golden crown on her head. Slowly she stretched her long neck,

lifted both wings, and a moment later she turned into a beautiful young woman – a princess, by the look of it, for the golden crown still glittered on her head.

Prince Siegfried had never seen anyone so beautiful, so elegant – and so haunted.

He stepped out of the shadows. "Do not be scared of me! I am Prince Siegfried."

The swan-maiden started. Her hands flew to her

face, but she did not cry out.

"I am Princess Odette," she whispered. "Please leave at once. If Rothbart sees you, he will surely put a curse on you."

"Rothbart?"

"He is an evil wizard, a magician. When I refused to marry him, he put a curse on me and my handmaidens. We are all doomed to spend the

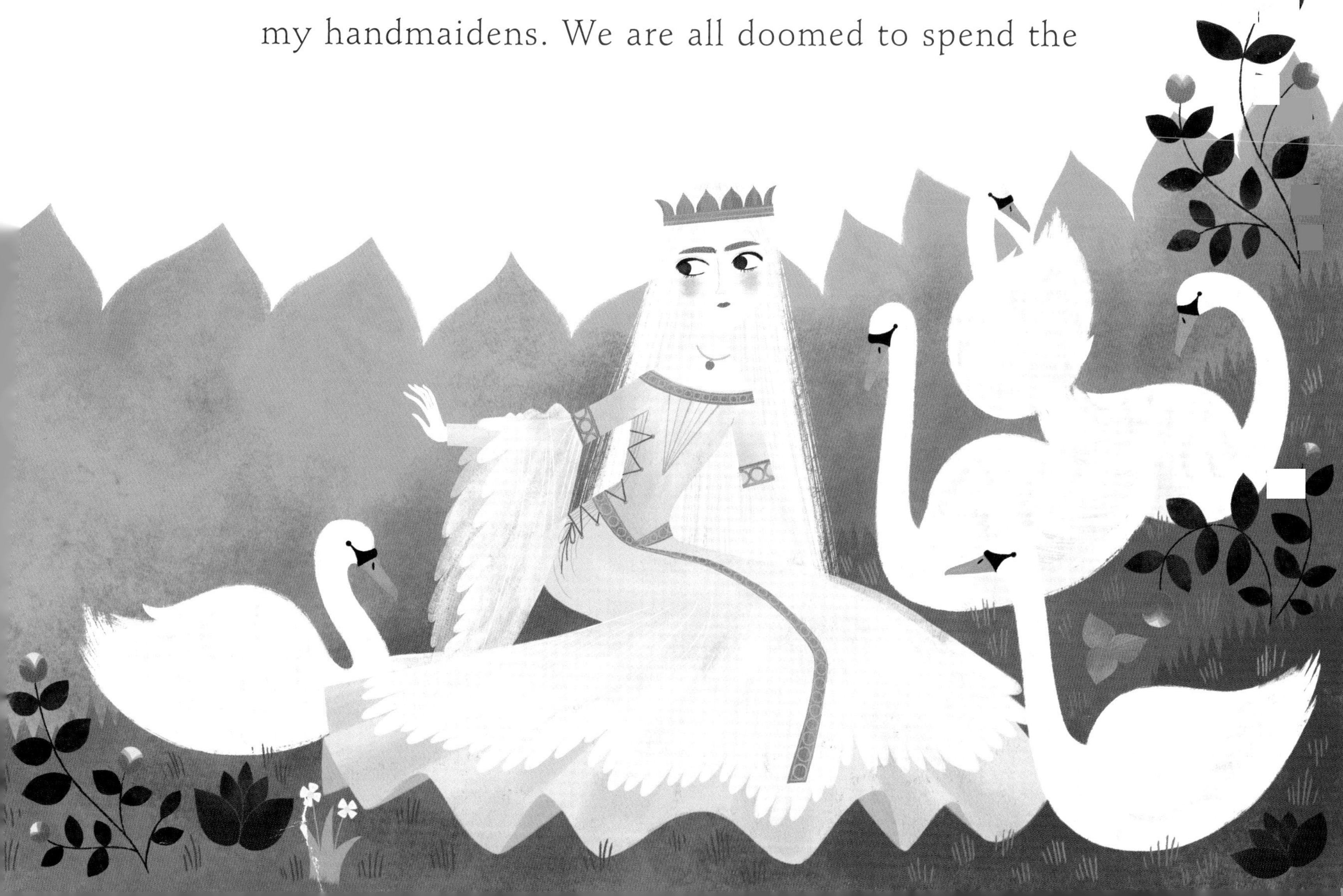

day in the shape of swans. Only at night do we turn back into girls. Then we come to this lake to dance. Rothbart made it from the tears my mother, shed when she knew I was cursed."

"Can't you escape your fate?" asked Siegfried.

"We are all cursed until a true prince promises to love me and only me," replied Odette.

"I shall find that evil Rothbart," hissed Siegfried, "and put an arrow through his heart."

Odette smiled sadly. "He follows us all night, disguised as an owl. But do not harm him. If he dies before the curse is lifted, my maidens and I will remain swans for ever."

The rest of the flock came ashore and, stretching their wings, they too became maidens. The older ones formed a circle around Odette and danced, the little cygnets following their movements. Prince Siegfried joined in, dancing with the princess.

Soon the sky began to pale. The night was over. An owl shrieked in the trees.

"That's Rothbart calling us," said Odette. "We must become swans once again."

"Come to my ball tonight," begged Prince Siegfried. "I shall choose you to be my wife. The spell will be broken and you and your maidens will be free."

"Hush," cried Odette. "Rothbart will hear you."

"Promise me you'll come."

"I will! I promise! But go now, please."

That evening at the ball, Prince Siegfried was introduced to one princess after another. The Princess Rosamunda of Spain! The Princess Isabella of Portugal! The Princess Esmeralda of Santa Fe!

Siegfried danced with every one of them, but his eye was continually on the door. Would Odette manage to give Rothbart the slip? Would she keep her promise and come?

"Well," said the queen, "which one of these beautiful

princesses is to be your lucky bride?"

"I refuse to choose," replied Siegfried, "until the sun has set."

His mother looked angry, but before she could say another word, there was a loud fanfare of trumpets. Another princess entered the ballroom, on the arm of an older man who was wearing a mask. She was dressed in black, with a glittering ruby at her throat.

"Odette! You came. Mother, this is Princess Odette."

"Princess who?" said his mother. "Do we know her family?"

The orchestra drowned out the rest of the queen's words. The dance floor filled with young people in fine clothes, all eager to dance, the girls doing their best to impress Prince Siegfried. But he only had eyes for Odette and would only dance with her. She danced even more gracefully than the night before, weaving a bright spell of happiness around him.

Had he looked away from her face, he might have glanced at the ballroom window, where a swan, frantic with worry, was beating her wings against the glass. What a pity he did not!

The music stopped and Prince Siegfried held up his hand to ask for silence. "I do not need to wait for sunset to choose a bride after all," he announced. "I have made my mind up already. I shall marry the Princess Odette."

He went down on one knee and kissed the princess's hand. "I promise to love you, and only you," he said.

"For ever?" asked the princess.

"For ever," replied Prince Siegfried.

The man who'd accompanied the princess ripped off his mask. It was Rothbart!

"You foolish boy! Do you think you can outwit me? The girl you have promised to love for ever is my daughter, Odile. I put a spell on her to make her look like Odette. The real Odette is still a swan. Look!" He pointed to the window, where the anguished swan was still beating her wings against the coloured panes.

"But I do not love your daughter," said Prince Siegfried.

"It does not matter. You have said the words. I wasn't able to share my life with Princess Odette, and neither will you."

The glass in the window cracked. The swan lifted her wings and took off into the dusk.

Prince Siegfried dashed out of the palace. "Odette, wait," he cried. "I was tricked. It is you I love, only you." He ran through the woods, searching for the

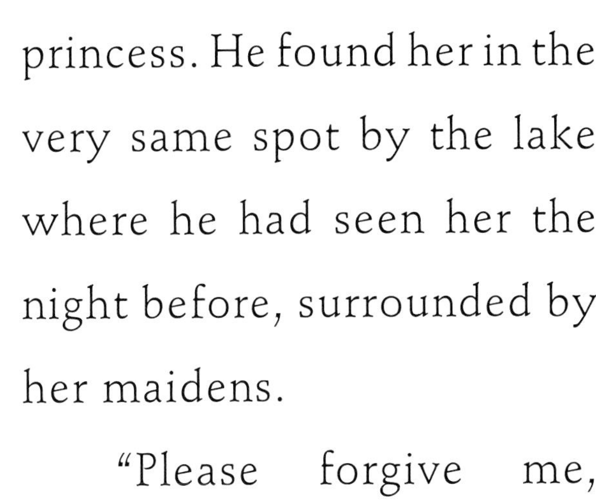

princess. He found her in the very same spot by the lake where he had seen her the night before, surrounded by her maidens.

"Please forgive me, Odette," said Siegfried.

"There is nothing to forgive – you were tricked. But the words you said to Odile cannot be unsaid. We will never be together."

"Perhaps not here, in my father's kingdom," said Prince Siegfried. "Perhaps not in this world. But we can be together somewhere else. Come!"

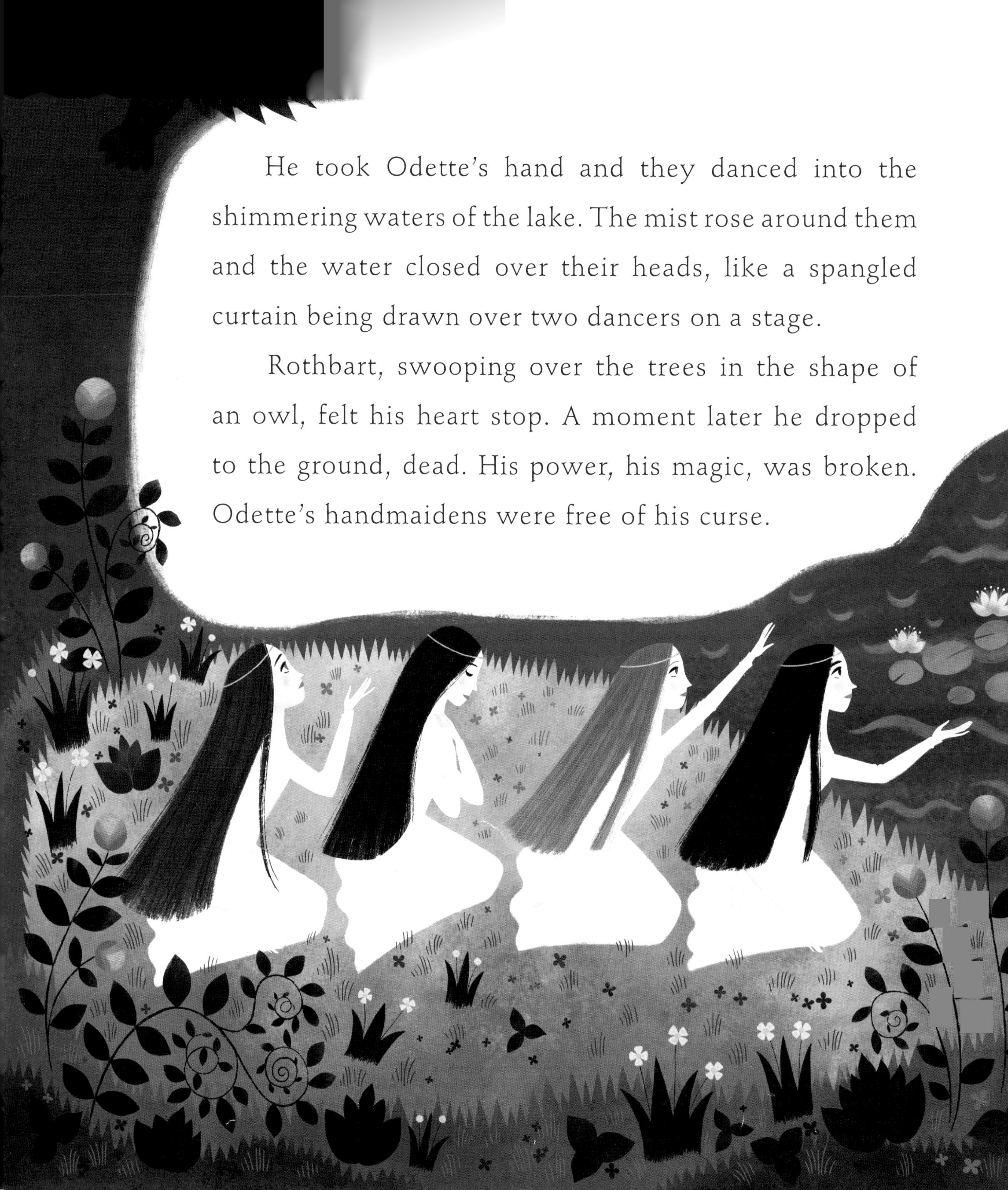

He took Odette's hand and they danced into the shimmering waters of the lake. The mist rose around them and the water closed over their heads, like a spangled curtain being drawn over two dancers on a stage.

Rothbart, swooping over the trees in the shape of an owl, felt his heart stop. A moment later he dropped to the ground, dead. His power, his magic, was broken. Odette's handmaidens were free of his curse.

It is said Prince Siegfried and Princess Odette dance at the bottom of the lake still, for true love always finds a way, and a princess can never be separated from a prince who truly loves her.

# The Firebird

IN THE MIDDLE OF A DARK wood stood an enchanted castle, cold and dreary, always in shadow. It had a garden but no flowers grew in it, only thorns. The path between the gate and the front door was littered with huge lumps of stone. They had strange shapes, like statues someone had forgotten to finish. Spiders had wrapped the stones in thick webs and toads crouched beneath them.

The trees outside the gate had been chopped down, leaving only stumps and gorse. Just one tree still stood: an apple tree too precious to cut down, for its fruit was made of solid gold.

One evening there was a rustle in the gorse. The spiders froze in their webs and the toads scuttled back under the strange boulders. A young man peered out from the woods. He was Prince Ivan, and he was looking for his friends who were out picking wild moonflowers.

*What a dismal place*, thought the prince. He explored the strange clearing, running his fingers along the boulders and trying the large handle on the gate.

Then he saw the golden apples on the tree! Before he could open the gate, a flash of colour in the night sky caught his eye. He ducked behind a fallen tree to watch. A moment later, something bright and searing swooped down from the sky, like a flame shot out of a dragon's mouth. It was a Firebird, her glowing red feathers dazzling the prince's eyes.

The creature settled on the grass only for a second. Then she was off again, half dancing, half flying around the clearing, closer and closer to the tree with the golden apples. The moment she got close enough, the prince pounced. "Got you!"

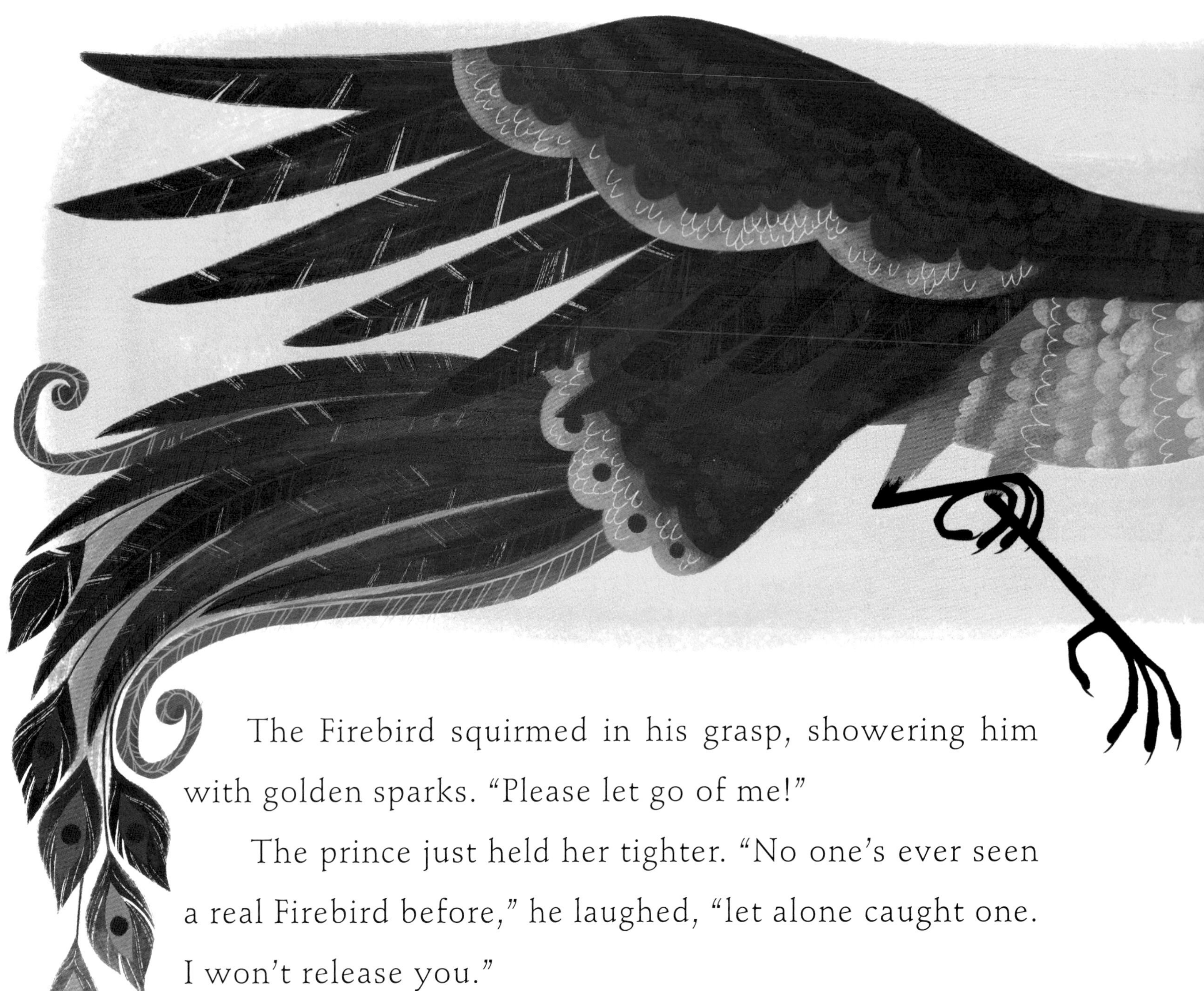

The Firebird squirmed in his grasp, showering him with golden sparks. “Please let go of me!”

The prince just held her tighter. “No one’s ever seen a real Firebird before,” he laughed, “let alone caught one. I won’t release you.”

“Keeping me captive will only bring you bad luck,” pleaded the Firebird. “Set me free and I shall give you a rare gift.”

"What kind of gift?"

The Firebird arched her neck and plucked the brightest feather from her tail. "If you are ever in trouble, wave this in the air and I shall come to your rescue."

"A generous gift indeed. Thank you."

Prince Ivan let go of the Firebird, and, spreading her wings, she swooped up into the night sky, leaving a trail of fire behind her like a comet.

The prince looked at the feather in his hand, glowing with fire and magic. He was just tucking it safely into his pocket when he heard voices behind him. The gate to the castle swung open. Quick as lightning, the prince dived back behind the fallen tree.

A long line of girls came out of the castle. The prince counted thirteen of them, all beautifully dressed in satin skirts, their necks decked with diamonds and rubies. Each girl wore a tiara on her head, and Ivan guessed that they must be princesses.

The last girl shut the gate behind them. She seemed a bit older than the rest, and her tiara had more jewels.

"Quiet, please," she warned the others, "or we'll be caught and punished."

"Yes, Princess Vasilisa."

"Let's play a game. How about hide-and-seek?" She tossed a golden apple from the tree to her friends. One girl caught it and began counting while Vasilisa and the others ran to find hiding places.

"Oh!" Princess Vasilisa had squeezed behind the fallen tree where Prince Ivan was crouched. "You are in danger, sir. If I were you, I would leave right away," she said.

"In danger?"

"From Kashchei," said the princess, "the evil wizard who kidnapped us and took us away from our families. He owns the castle."

She nodded at the boulders behind the gate. "They were once men like you. Men foolish enough to come searching for us. Kashchei caught them and turned them to solid rock. He would turn us princesses into stone too, except he needs us to look after the castle."

"I am not afraid of anyone," said Prince Ivan. "Not even an evil wizard who can turn people to stone."

The princess smiled at his foolishness, and the prince noticed she had dazzling eyes, as dazzling as the Firebird's feathers.

"Please go home before you're caught. I can tell by your fine outfit that you are a prince. Your subjects, not to mention your family, would miss you if you were turned to stone."

But Prince Ivan refused to leave. He insisted on staying to join in with the games and watch the princesses dance.

All too soon, the birds in the woods started to chirp their morning song.

"We must go back indoors," Princess Vasilisa told Prince Ivan. "Goodbye, sir."

"Wait," said Prince Ivan. "Will you come out again tomorrow?" He followed the princesses, eager for an answer.

"Take great care!" warned Princess Vasilisa. "You must not venture into the wizard's garden . . . "

But it was too late! Prince Ivan had already stepped past the gate. Alarm bells rang out in the castle. The door flew open and out swarmed a rabble of ogres and trolls, all leering and grinning and prodding the air with their swords. They flowed around Prince Ivan like a black tide, pushing the princess and her friends away, dragging him across the garden to the castle door.

A tall creature, an old man, emerged from the castle. He stood in front of Prince Ivan, framed by a fiery light. His face was a grinning skull; his eyes sparkled like black diamonds. He brandished fingernails as long and sharp as daggers. In his hand, he held a walking stick, its head carved into a flying crow.

"Welcome to my castle! I am Kashchei the Deathless. And who might you be?"

The Prince held his head high. "My name is Prince

Ivan. I might not have magic powers, but I am not afraid of you. I order you to release me, and let these young ladies go too."

"A prince, do you say?" chuckled Kashchei. "I don't believe I have a prince in my collection. Yet!"

"Please," called out Princess Vasilisa from behind the rabble of ogres, "let him go. Turn me to stone instead!"

Kashchei ignored her. Muttering a strange chant, he raised his hands and pointed his dagger-like fingers at Prince Ivan. The prince, struggling in the ogres' grasp, felt his feet turn numb. His arms grew heavy. He had no idea if it was fear or Kashchei's magic that was robbing him of his strength, but he knew there was only one thing that would save him now. He reached into his pocket and drew out the glowing feather.

Kashchei laughed. "Fool! Do you think a bird will be a match for my powerful magic?"

But there, swooping once more out of the sky, was the Firebird, answering the prince's call. She alighted on the grass and her glow filled the night, dazzling the ogres and the trolls.

She looked straight at Kashchei. "Let's see whose magic is more powerful. Dance with me, you wicked fool, and let your monsters dance with you."

The Firebird began to dance. Immediately, Kashchei's feet leapt up from under him and he started dancing too, following the Firebird round the clearing. His face turned purple with rage but he couldn't stop. The ogres and monsters found themselves dancing behind him. Round and round they stomped, churning up the mud with their boots. They kept on moving, unable to stop, till one by one they fell to the ground, exhausted.

"If you have a soul, let the princesses go," Prince Ivan shouted at Kashchei, who had collapsed by the castle gate.

"Ah, but the wizard's soul is not inside him," whispered the Firebird. "He has hidden it somewhere to protect it. Somewhere close by, where he can keep an eye on it. Somewhere a brave prince can find it . . ."

Prince Ivan began frantically searching the woods, running from tree to tree, feeling inside hollow

trunks. At last his hands closed round a jewelled box hidden between the roots of an oak. He turned the key and opened it. A huge egg lay inside, nestled in golden straw.

"Be careful with that, you little wretch." The wizard reared up from the ground where he lay, his hands raking the air.

Now Ivan knew for sure that the egg contained Kashchei's soul. He raised it high above his head and hurled it to the ground, smashing it to pieces.

A flash of angry fire rose into the air. Then the wizard roared in pain, clutching his chest. His eyes bulged. His long fingernails curled up and melted like wax. A moment later he collapsed in a heap of dry bones, which turned to dust and were blown away by the wind. The trolls and ogres faded into whispering shadows.

Slowly, the lumps of stone on the path turned back into people. They stretched to remove years of stiffness from their hands and legs.

"We are free! Free!" they cried.

They gathered round Prince Ivan to thank him. The princesses crowded round too. They could go home now, back to their families, their parents, their lives.

A trumpet blared across the woods. The prince's friends had found him at last.

"Will you come with me to my palace?" Prince Ivan asked the Princess Vasilisa. "Will you marry me?"

"Only if you promise never to go chasing Firebirds across the woods again," she laughed.

At the wedding, the princess wore a crown made of golden apples, picked from the tree outside Kashchei's garden.

The Firebird was the guest of honour. She danced to entertain everyone, whirling higher and higher into the clouds until she disappeared.

Who knows if she left the prince a second feather, just in case?

# Cinderella

I *WISH I COULD GO to the prince's ball tonight*, thought Cinderella as she scrubbed the kitchen floor. There was no chance of that happening, of course. Her stepsisters, Nosy and Bossy, were going with their mother. But not Cinderella! Ever since her own mother died and her father remarried, she'd done nothing but cook and clean and wait on her stepsisters hand and foot.

How Cinderella wished her father were here now. He would never let anyone be mean to her, and he would surely let Cinderella go to the ball. But he was far away on a long journey, while Cinderella was stuck at home, cleaning up after Nosy and Bossy.

Cinderella's stepsisters were always fighting and arguing. Right now they were quarrelling over a shawl.

"I'm going to wear it!" screamed Bossy, yanking the shawl one way.

"It goes better with MY dress!" shouted Nosy, pulling it

the other way. There was a loud ripping noise as the shawl was torn in two.

"Now look what you've done!" cried Bossy.

"You tore it, not me," Nosy fumed. "I'll tell Mama not to let you come to the ball. I don't know why you're coming anyway. The prince will never dance with you. You move like a hippopotamus."

"Well, you've got a face like a horse," said Bossy. "I will dance with the prince tonight and I won't be surprised if he falls in love with me. He's sure to ask me to marry him."

"Nonsense," snapped Nosy. "He'll only have eyes for ME!"

"Stop fighting, girls," said their mother. "Remember, real ladies don't bicker."

Suddenly, there was a loud knock at the kitchen door.

"Hurry up and answer it, Cinderella," said Bossy.

An old woman stood on the doorstep, shivering in the cold. "Pity a hungry beggar, my lady," she said.

"Not another poor person," moaned Bossy.

"She's probably a thief in disguise," added Nosy.

"Send the beggar away, Cinderella," ordered her stepmother. "And come and iron my stockings at once. Hurry up!"

"Here, take this," Cinderella whispered. She thrust a piece of bread she had been saving for her own supper into the old woman's chapped hands.

"Thank you, my lady," said the beggar. "May all your wishes come true."

*I'd be happy if just one wish came true*, thought Cinderella as she closed the door. *It must be wonderful to dance with a prince.*

There was more knocking at the door. A glove-maker brought gloves for the sisters and a wig-maker delivered wigs. A handsome dance teacher came to make sure the two sisters remembered the steps he'd taught them. Nosy and Bossy fought over which one of them was to hold his hand the longest.

At last it was time to go to the ball. Cinderella's stepmother hurried Nosy and Bossy into a coach waiting outside.

"Now, Cinderella, make sure you tidy the kitchen while we're gone," she said. "And chop up some firewood too." And with that she climbed into the coach and the three of them set off for the palace.

Cinderella was left alone in the kitchen with a pile of dishes to wash and a dirty floor to clean. She picked up the broom, but instead of sweeping, she started dancing round and round the kitchen. A picture of her mother, framed over the mantelpiece, caught her eye.

"Oh, Mama, if you were still alive, I'm sure you'd let me go to the ball . . . "

Suddenly Cinderella heard a voice behind her: "But you *will* go to the ball! For it is not jewels and crowns that make a princess, but the kindness of her heart."

A dark shadow moved across the floor and there was the beggar woman, back in the kitchen, even though the door was closed and the bolt drawn. Her eyes twinkled mischievously.

"Your kindness to a hungry woman shall be rewarded," she said. She held up her right hand and a magic wand appeared in her fingers. Her rags turned into a beautiful dress, covered in shimmering leaves and stars and snowflakes.

"I am your fairy godmother, Cinderella," said the woman. "It was your mother's dying wish that I look after you. So I shall send you to the ball."

She waved her wand and at once a fire leapt up in the hearth. Out of the flames skipped four fairies, dancing on gossamer wings. The first was a spring fairy dressed in blossoming flowers. The second, a summer fairy dressed in sunshine and sea spray. The third was

an autumn fairy clothed in velvet-soft leaves. And the last was a winter fairy with a dress made of sparkling snowflakes.

The fairies had brought gifts for Cinderella, which they laid at her feet.

A bunch of snowdrops from the spring fairy!

A golden lizard from the summer fairy!

A big, round pumpkin from the autumn fairy!

And six white mice from the winter fairy!

"These are strange gifts!" laughed Cinderella.

"These gifts have a purpose," replied her fairy godmother. She tapped each one of them in turn with her wand, and Cinderella watched in amazement as the lizard turned into a horse, the mice into footmen and the pumpkin into a dazzling coach.

Last of all, the fairy godmother touched the snowdrops, and all at once Cinderella was dressed in a beautiful

white ball gown. Rings appeared on her fingers, bracelets jangled on her wrists and a tiara crowned her head.

"But you mustn't go to the ball barefoot, my dear," said the fairy godmother, looking at Cinderella's feet. Then, reaching deep into the folds of her dress, she pulled out a pair of shoes that sparkled in the firelight. They were beautiful glass dancing shoes, as dainty as dewdrops on a spider's web. The fairies took the shoes and slipped them on to Cinderella's feet.

"These will help you dance like a princess, my dear," said her fairy godmother. "But be careful. My magic will wear off at midnight. Make sure you come home before then."

*

At the palace, Nosy and Bossy were making fools of themselves, trying to impress two lords who'd agreed to dance with them. Nosy was stepping on her partner's toes, while Bossy was kicking hers in the shins.

Suddenly the orchestra stopped playing. A late arrival was dancing into the ballroom. She was so beautiful and so graceful, she seemed to be floating. The prince, who had been busy trying to avoid dancing with Nosy and Bossy, stepped forward and held out his hand.

"Welcome to my party."

"It's so rude of me to be late," replied the new guest. "Please forgive me, Your Royal Highness."

"There is nothing to forgive," replied the prince. "Will you dance with me?"

The mysterious princess was none other than Cinderella.

She looked so beautiful in her ballgown, her stepsisters did not recognise her.

Cinderella and the prince danced together all night long. Around them, the other girls glared and whispered to each other behind their fans.

"Who is she?"

"Where did she come from?"

"Where does one get such a beautiful dress?" Bossy sighed. "I would look beautiful too, if Mama could get hold of such a dress for me."

"Ha, you'd look like a donkey whatever you wore," snorted Nosy.

"Be nice to each other, girls," said their mother.

Just then, right in the middle of a dance, the clock began to chime.

"What time is it?" gasped Cinderella.

"Midnight," murmured the prince.

"Midnight! I promised my godmother I'd be home by midnight."

Cinderella pulled back from the prince, and suddenly she was running to the door.

"Wait!" called the prince, running after her. "Can I send a coach for you tomorrow? Will you come again?"

But Cinderella did not answer. The prince watched as she dashed down the steps of the palace. She was in such a rush, she did not even notice that one of her glass dancing shoes had slipped off her foot.

The prince picked up the shoe. "I shall only dance with the girl whose foot fits into this shoe," he said. "And, if she'll have me, I'll marry her . . . "

Cinderella woke up by the fire at home, dressed in her old rags, the broomstick still in her hands. What a dream she'd had! The old beggar turning out to be her fairy godmother! Going to the prince's ball in a coach! Wearing a beautiful gown and glass dancing shoes! Dancing with the prince himself!

Bossy and Nosy burst into the kitchen, followed by their mother. Their faces were purple with anger.

"The prince refused to dance with me."

"And me."

"He'd only dance with that stupid princess who floats," fumed Bossy. "He's going to marry her too, if he can find her. He stopped the ball to go looking for her."

"The prince swore he'd marry the girl whose foot fits into that silly dancing shoe," Nosy corrected her. "There's a difference. Perhaps it will fit on my foot . . . "

"Or mine," said Bossy.

A loud fanfare of trumpets sounded outside the door. "His Majesty is here!" cried the girls' mother. She opened the door, bowing her head so low she nearly scraped it on the floor. A footman entered, carrying Cinderella's glass dancing shoe on a satin cushion. The prince came in behind him, stopping in the doorway.

"His Royal Highness the Prince is travelling all around the land in the hope of finding the young woman whose foot fits this shoe," said the footman. He held the cushion towards Nosy. "Would you care to try the shoe on, my lady?"

Nosy grabbed the glass shoe with both hands. "I should imagine it's in my size . . . " She scrunched up her toes so hard they turned bright purple. Even so, her foot was far too big to fit into the shoe.

Bossy snatched it from her. "Give it to me, you elephant. Let me try it on." She huffed and puffed and squashed and squeezed, but the dancing shoe still did not fit.

"Oh, the stupid thing has shrunk in the rain," she cried. "It's stuck! Cinderella, help me get the wretched thing off . . . "

Cinderella rushed forward, and, as she bent to help Bossy, something tumbled out of her apron pocket. It was the other dancing shoe!

The footman made a dive for it and handed it to the prince.

The prince looked at Cinderella. "It's you!" he gasped.

"YOU?" cried Bossy.

"Don't be daft, your royal handsomeness," said Nosy. "Cinderella is just our lazy, ugly, good-for-nothing stepsister."

Cinderella smiled shyly at the prince. "I am sorry I ran away, Your Majesty. My fairy godmother's spell ended at midnight. I did not want you to see me in rags."

"What rags?" said the prince.

Cinderella held up her tattered sleeves to show him . . . only to find that the fairy godmother had worked her magic again. She was dressed in the same beautiful clothes she had worn to the ball.

"It does not matter to me whether you are dressed in silk or in rags," said the prince. "I love you, and I believe you love me. Will you be my princess and marry me? Will you come to live with me in my palace?"

"I will," said Cinderella, "but only if my father can come too, when he returns home from his travels. And we shall have to take my stepmother as well, for he will be lonely without her. I would like to bring my stepsisters with me too, for though they are rude, deep down in their hearts they are really kind."

And so Cinderella put on her dancing shoes

and danced with her prince all the way to the royal palace. It was no less than she deserved, for as her fairy godmother had said, it is not jewels and crowns that make a princess, but the kindness of her heart.

# The Nutcracker

OLD UNCLE DROSSELMEYER was a superb toymaker, a magician and a fabulous storyteller who'd been to every country in the world. Oh, but he was always late! He didn't get to Clara and Fritz's Christmas party till the dancing had started, and then he appeared in a cloud of green smoke, like a conjuror on a stage.

“Happy Christmas, everyone,” he roared. His servants wheeled in a bright red box, as big as a wardrobe. Uncle Drosselmeyer threw open the doors and out stepped two wooden dancers, as big as real people, and just as graceful in their movements.

He’d brought Christmas gifts for everyone. Hobbyhorses for all the children! A new clock for the mantelpiece! An angel to go on top of the Christmas tree! A box of soldiers for Fritz! And, for his goddaughter,

Clara, a splendid nutcracker doll.

"Thank you, Uncle Drosselmeyer," gasped Clara. "What a handsome nutcracker he is."

"Let me see if it works," said her brother, Fritz. He grabbed the nutcracker – and it broke in two!

"Fritz, you brute!" cried Clara.

Uncle Drosselmeyer picked up the two pieces, flourished his scarf over them and – hey presto! – the nutcracker was repaired.

Clara put him away in the china cabinet for safekeeping. He stood proudly between the teapot and the sauceboat, watching the dancing.

All too soon the clock struck ten, bringing the party to a close. The dinner table was cleared, the candles on the Christmas tree blown out and the curtains drawn. The children went to bed, stuffed full of Christmas pudding and happiness, and soon everyone was asleep.

Everyone except Clara. She couldn't sleep. She tossed and turned under the blankets, counting sheep, but she couldn't stop thinking about the nutcracker. It was so quiet in the house, surely it would do no harm if she crept downstairs and had one more look in the china cabinet?

But when she reached the drawing room, Clara found that the nutcracker was gone. Perhaps Fritz had stolen him, or perhaps Uncle Drosselmeyer had decided to make sure he had been repaired properly . . .

Just at that moment, the new clock on the mantelpiece struck midnight. The angel on the Christmas tree fluttered her wings. The candles started to glow again and the baubles sparkled. The Christmas tree began to grow bigger and bigger, its scented branches reaching out across the room.

Clara heard the sound of a bugle, followed by a shout: “Get him, soldiers!” Out of the darkness leapt a crowd of mice, as tall as Clara herself, each one brandishing a sword.

The mice ignored Clara and swarmed around the china cabinet, which had magically changed into a castle. The drawbridge came down, and out stepped the Nutcracker, now as tall as the mice themselves.

He was followed by Fritz's toy soldiers.

"Charge, men!" cried the Nutcracker.

"Take the castle," called one of the mice, who had a crown on his head. He was obviously the Mouse King, and very fierce he looked too, with his enormous whiskers and long tail.

A battle broke out in the living room, the mice thrusting with their swords and the Nutcracker's men firing their rifles. They were very brave, those young men, but there had

only been ten soldiers in Uncle Drosselmeyer's box and there were a lot of mice. Soon the mice had the Nutcracker cornered.

"Do you surrender?" demanded the Mouse King.

"No, he does not!" shouted Clara, standing up on the sofa. She took off one of her slippers and threw it at the Mouse King. It hit him on the head! The king dropped to the floor and the other mice gathered around him. In a jiffy they had whisked him off through a giant mouse hole in the skirting board.

The Nutcracker turned to Clara. "Thank you, my lady. You have saved my men and set me free."

"Free?" said Clara.

"I am really a prince," said the Nutcracker. "My mother is a queen. She angered the Mouse King by setting mousetraps all around the kitchen. He took his revenge by turning me into a Nutcracker. I was to remain a wooden doll until a girl broke the spell by helping me win in battle. My mother turned to your Uncle Drosselmeyer for help. He is a frequent visitor to our kingdom, the enchanted Land of Sweets."

"A prince," murmured Clara. "A land of sweets . . . "

"You must meet my mother," said the prince. "I am sure she would like to thank you personally for breaking the spell."

As he spoke, the angel on the Christmas tree fluttered her wings once more. A gust of wind blew the windows open and the living room was suddenly full of whirling snowflakes. The Christmas tree, the sofa, the china cabinet and everything in the room melted away. A sleigh, drawn by two snow-white reindeer, appeared out of nowhere. The prince lifted Clara into it, and they took off into the sky, the snowflakes dancing around them.

It must have been hours, or perhaps it was minutes – Clara was so busy looking around her, she lost all track of time – before they alighted in front of a palace. It seemed to be covered in icing, with lighted candles on the turrets.

"This is my home," the prince told Clara.

People came out of the castle to greet them: liquorice soldiers in cherry-red uniforms; dukes and duchesses with candyfloss hair and little children with faces as round as lollipops. Last of all came the queen: the Sugarplum Fairy.

The crown on her head was made of spun sugar that glittered brightly in the moonlight, and her wand was a stick of rock, topped with a marzipan star.

"Mother," said the prince, "this is Clara."

"Thank you for bringing my son home safely." The Sugarplum Fairy smiled. "We had word from Mr Drosselmeyer that you were coming, so we have prepared a feast for you, and entertainment too."

Oh, and what a show it was! Performers from all over the world had gathered to entertain Clara. Dancers from China, the land of tea; from Arabia, the land of coffee; from Spain, the land of dark chocolate; and from Russia, the land of candy cane. The Sugarplum Fairy danced too, with her prince, the Cavalier.

Time flies by when you're having fun, and soon the

morning light appeared in the sky.

"You must make a wish before you go back home," the Sugarplum Fairy said to Clara.

"I wish . . . " said Clara, "I wish that I could come and visit you all again."

"Oh, but you will, my dear," replied the Sugarplum Fairy. "Have a happy Christmas, and we'll see you again . . . soon."

The prince kissed Clara's hand. "Yes," he whispered, "we'll see you again . . . soon."

Behind him, the Sugarplum Fairy waved her wand. The marzipan star twinkled, and Clara felt her eyelids grow heavy with sleep. When she opened them again, she was lying in her own bed. Fritz was shaking her awake, and the delicious smell of Christmas breakfast was wafting up from the kitchen downstairs. *It was all a dream*, she thought sadly. *Nothing but a dream!*

When she went downstairs, Clara saw that the Nutcracker was back in the china cabinet, standing to attention between the teapot and the sauceboat. She opened it to take him out, and there at his feet was . . . a marzipan star.